Chicago Bee Branch
3647 S. State Street
Chicago, IL 60609

A Note to Parents

Welcome to REAL KIDS READERS, a series of phonics-based books for children who are beginning to read. In the classroom, educators use phonics to teach children how to sound out unfamiliar words, providing a firm foundation for reading skills. At home, you can use REAL KIDS READERS to reinforce and build on that foundation, because the books follow the same basic phonic guidelines that children learn in school.

Of course the best way to help your child become a good reader is to make the experience fun—and REAL KIDS READERS do that, too. With their realistic story lines and lively characters, the books engage children's imaginations. With their clean design and sparkling photographs, they provide picture clues that help new readers decipher the text. The combination is sure to entertain young children and make them truly want to read.

REAL KIDS READERS have been developed at three distinct levels to make it easy for children to read at their own pace.

- LEVEL 1 is for children who are just beginning to read.
- LEVEL 2 is for children who can read with help.
- LEVEL 3 is for children who can read on their own.

A controlled vocabulary provides the framework at each level. Repetition, rhyme, and humor help increase word skills. Because children can understand the words and follow the stories, they quickly develop confidence. They go back to each book again and again, increasing their proficiency and sense of accomplishment, until they're ready to move on to the next level. The result is a rich and rewarding experience that will help them develop a lifelong love of reading.

To the greatest godchildren in the world—
Brian Baumann, Tara Pasqualone,
and Elizabeth Pollice—
thanks for all those proud moments
—L. V. T.

For Myles
—D. H.

Special thanks to Lands' End, Dodgeville, WI, for providing Tara's
clothing and to Mattituck Florist and Garden Shop, Mattituck, NY,
for providing gardening supplies.

Produced by DWAI / Seventeenth Street Productions, Inc.
Reading Specialist: Virginia Grant Clammer

Library of Congress Cataloging-in-Publication Data

Tidd, Louise.
    Let me help! / Louise Vitellaro Tidd ; photographs by Dorothy Handelman.
        p.   cm. — (Real kids readers. Level 2)
    Summary: Tara tries to help her father with his chores but only succeeds in making more
work for him.
    ISBN 0-7613-2067-9 (lib. bdg.). — ISBN 0-7613-2092-X (pbk.)
    [1. Helpfulness—Fiction. 2. Fathers and daughters—Fiction.] I. Handelman, Dorothy, ill.
II. Title. III. Series.
PZ7.T4345Le   1999
[E]—dc21   98-52515
                                                                                CIP
                                                                                AC

pbk: 10 9 8 7 6 5 4 3
lib: 10 9 8 7 6 5 4 3 2

Let Me Help!

By Louise Vitellaro Tidd
Photographs by Dorothy Handelman

M

The Millbrook Press

Brookfield, Connecticut

Dad has a lot to do today.
He makes a list of his jobs.

Tara wants to help.
"What will you do first?" she asks.

THINGS TO DO

1) Put books on shelf.
2) Plant seeds.
3) Put away clothes.
4) Paint wall.
5) Go to store.

"I will put all these books away,"
says Dad.
"That's not hard," says Tara.
"Let me help."
"Be careful," says Dad. "Don't rush."

7

Now Dad has to plant seeds.
Tara wants to help.
She lifts the bag of dirt.
"Be careful," says Dad.
"That bag is heavy."

The bag falls to the floor.
"Oh, no!" says Tara. "What a mess!"
She feels bad.
But Dad says, "No harm done.
We can clean this up together."
They sweep up all the dirt.
Then they plant the seeds in the pots
and water them.

13

"Now I'll put away the clothes,"
says Dad.
"I know where they go," says Tara.
"Let me help."

"Wait, Tara," says Dad.
"That basket is too big for you."
But Tara wants to help.
She tries to carry all the clothes.

The basket tips and falls.
"Oh, no!" says Tara.
"The clothes fell on the pots.
Now they are dirty!"

"Oh, well," says Dad.
"We can clean this up together."
They wash and dry the clothes.
Then they put them away.

"Time to paint the wall," says Dad.
He gets out the things he needs.
"Wow!" says Tara. "I love to paint.
Let me help."
"Wait, Tara!" says Dad.
"I don't think you can reach the paint."
Tara tries anyway—and the paint spills.
Splash!

Tara starts to cry.
"Now look what I did!" she sobs.

"I really want to help.
But all I do is make messes."
"Don't feel bad," says Dad.
"We can clean this up together."
He gives Tara a hug.
"I'm glad you want to help," he says.
"You just have to slow down
and be more careful."

Tara and Dad clean up the mess.
He paints the wall.
Then they go to the store.
Tara helps get the food they need.
She doesn't rush.
She doesn't try to pick up
things that are too heavy,
or too big,
or out of reach.

When they get home,
Tara opens the door for Dad.
He brings in two bags of food.
"Wait, Dad," says Tara.
"Those bags look heavy."
"It's okay," says Dad.
"I can carry them."

The bags slip from Dad's hands.
Crash!
They hit the floor.

"Oh, no!" he says. "What a mess!
Maybe I should slow down
and be more careful too."

Tara gives Dad a hug.
"It's okay. Don't feel bad," she says.
"We can clean this up together."

Phonic Guidelines

Use the following guidelines to help your child read the words in *Let Me Help!*

Short Vowels

When two consonants surround a vowel, the sound of the vowel is usually short. This means you pronounce *a* as in apple, *e* as in egg, *i* as in igloo, *o* as in octopus, and *u* as in umbrella. Short-vowel words in this story include: *bad, bag, big, but, can, Dad, did, get, has, his, hit, hug, jobs, let, lot, not, sobs, tips.*

Short-Vowel Words with Consonant Blends

When two or more different consonants are side by side, they usually blend to make a combined sound. In this story, short-vowel words with consonant blends include: *brings, bumps, glad, hands, help, just, lifts, list, plant, slip, spills.*

Double Consonants

When two identical consonants appear side by side, one of them is silent. In this story, double consonants appear in the short-vowel words *kiss* and *tell*, and in the *all*-family words *all, falls, wall.*

R-Controlled Vowels

When a vowel is followed by the letter *r*, its sound is changed by the *r*. In this story, words with *r*-controlled vowels include: *are, dirt, first, for, hard, harm, more, starts.*

Long Vowel and Silent E

If a word has a vowel and ends with an *e*, usually the vowel is long and the *e* is silent. Long vowels are pronounced the same way as their alphabet names. In this story, words with a long vowel and silent *e* include: *home, late, make, store, time.*

Double Vowels

When two vowels are side by side, usually the first vowel is long and the second vowel is silent. Double-vowel words in this story include: *clean, feel, need, paint, seeds, sweep, wait.*

Diphthongs

Sometimes when two vowels (or a vowel and a consonant) are side by side, they combine to make a diphthong—a sound that is different from long or short vowel sounds. Diphthongs are: *au/aw, ew, oi/oy, ou/ow*. In this story, words with diphthongs include: *down, now, out, wow.*

Consonant Digraphs

Sometimes when two different consonants are side by side, they make a digraph that represents a single new sound. Consonant digraphs are: *ch, sh, th, wh*. In this story, words with digraphs include: *crash, reach, rush, that, then, these, they, things, this, those, wash, what, where.*

Silent Consonants

Sometimes when two different consonants appear side by side, one of them is silent. In this story, words with silent consonants include: *know, pick.*

Sight Words

Sight words are those words that a reader must learn to recognize immediately—by sight—instead of by sounding them out. They occur with high frequency in easy texts. Sight words not included in the above categories are: *a, and, asks, away, be, do, gives, go, have, he, I, in, into, is, it, look, love, me, no, of, okay, put, says, she, the, to, too, two, up, wants, we, you.*